READ ALL THESE

NATE THE GREAT DETECTIVE STORIES

AND CONTINUE THE DETECTIVE FUN WITH

OLIVIA SHARP

by Marjorie Weinman Sharmat and Mitchell Sharmat
illustrated by Denise Brunkus

Nate the Great

Where Are You?

by

Marjorie Weinman Sharmat
and Mitchell Sharmat

illustrated by Jody Wheeler
in the style of Marc Simont

Delacorte Press

Text copyright © 2014 by Marjorie Weinman Sharmat and Mitchell Sharmat
New illustrations of Nate the Great, Sludge, Rosamond, Annie, Claude, Harry, Fang, and the Hexes by Jody Wheeler based upon the original drawings by Marc Simont. All other images copyright © 2014 by Jody Wheeler.

Visit us on the Web! randomhouse.com/kids

Educators and librarians, for a variety of teaching tools, visit us at RHTeachersLibrarians.com

Library of Congress Cataloging-in-Publication Data
Sharmat, Marjorie Weinman, author.
Nate the Great, where are you? / by Marjorie Weinman Sharmat and Mitchell Sharmat ; illustrated by Jody Wheeler in the style of Marc Simont. — First edition.
pages cm
Summary: "Nate the Great and his dog, Sludge, would like to take a break from detective work, but new cases—cases they do not want—await them" — Provided by publisher.
ISBN 978-0-385-74336-5 (hardback) — ISBN 978-0-375-99109-7 (glb)
ISBN 978-0-449-81077-4 (ebook)
[1. Mystery and detective stories. 2. Dogs—Fiction.] I. Sharmat, Mitchell, author. II. Wheeler, Jody, illustrator. III. Simont, Marc, illustrator. IV. Title.
PZ7.S5299Naz 2014
[Fic]—dc23
2013028764

The text of this book is set in 17-point Goudy Old Style.

Book design by Trish Parcell

Printed in the United States of America

10 9 8 7 6 5 4 3 2 1

First Edition

From Mitchell and Marjorie

Chapter One

Too Many Cases

My name is Nate the Great.
I am a detective.
My dog, Sludge, is a detective too.
We have been together
for a long time.
We have been eating pancakes and bones
and solving cases together.
Sludge wasn't on my first case.
But he has been with me
on all my cases
since the day I found him in a field.

Sometimes we have too many cases.
Today I was eating pancakes.
Sludge was crunching a bone.
"Eating is the best part of the day," I said.
"Today we have five cases I do not want.
And you do not want.
Listen!"
Sludge's ears pricked up.
"First case," I said.
"Rosamond asked me
to find her missing turnip.
She said it ran away.

Second case: Annie said
she couldn't find Fang's
special dog toothpaste.
'It makes Fang's teeth look
big and shiny and hungry,'
she said.

Third case: Claude, who is
always losing things, just
told me that he won't
have anything special
to find today.
'You are a great detective,'
Claude said.
'Find me something great to find.
Something really, really special.'

Fourth case . . ."
Sludge looked bored.
"Too many cases," I said.
"And Rosamond, Annie,
Fang, Claude, and Harry
are all after us," I said.
"We must escape."

I wrote a note to my mother.

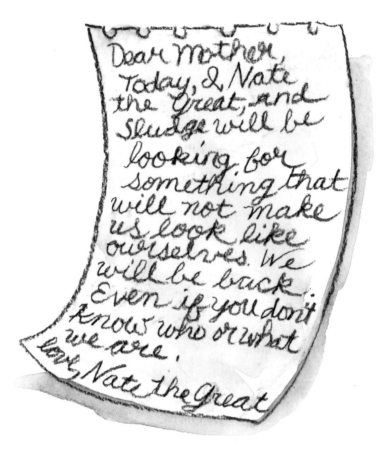

Dear Mother,
Today, I, Nate the Great, and Sludge will be looking for something that will not make us look like ourselves. We will be back. Even if you don't know who or what we are.
Love, Nate the Great

Sludge and I walked out the back door.
"We are going to the Disguises for
Detectives store," I said.
"We will walk fast."

Chapter Two

The Perfect Disguise

Soon we were at the store.
"I am Nate the Great.
I am a detective," I said to the man
behind the counter.
"Today I have five cases.
Today I don't want to look like
Nate the Great.
Sludge here is also a detective."
"He looks like a dog," the man said.
"I agree. But don't you have
disguises for dog detectives?"

"Well, I have this soft scarf
with three fluffy tails.
It will be a fine disguise for your dog.
Here, I'll put it on him."
Sludge was excited.
He wagged his four tails.
Then he bit the three fluffy ones.
"I might possibly be able
to make him look like a cat,"
the man said.
Sludge bit again.

"Do you have anything for me?"
I asked.
The man brought out a costume.
"You will be from Mars," he said.
"I, Nate the Great, say that Mars
is not in my neighborhood.
Neither is a four-tailed dog.
We would be noticed right away."

The man suddenly smiled.

"Wait," he said.

"I have something perfect.

Trees are in our neighborhood.

I have a new tree costume for you.

And your dog detective

would look fine as a bush.

And green is such a lovely color.

You and your dog were meant for green."

Sludge sniffed and sniffed the bush costume.

Was he trying to tell me something?
Did he think he should be a bush?
Sludge is not prickly.
Sludge is not shedding leaves.
"Thank you anyway," I said to the man.
"We'll be back for Halloween."

Chapter Three
Out of Sight

"Let's take a walk in the woods,"
I said to Sludge.
We rushed into the woods
and found a bench
that was surrounded
by bushes and trees and flowers.
"Nobody can see us here," I said.
Sludge wagged his one and only tail.
He was happy.
"It's nice and quiet, too," I said.
"This will be a perfect day."

Suddenly we heard a loud voice.

A strange loud voice.

"NATE THE GREAT, WHERE ARE YOU?"

Rosamond was calling.

Rosamond has a strange voice.

Rosamond has a strange everything.

Then I heard more voices.

"NATE THE GREAT, WHERE ARE YOU?"
"NATE THE GREAT, WHERE ARE YOU?"
"NATE THE GREAT, WHERE ARE YOU?"
"NATE THE GREAT, WHERE ARE YOU?"
Suddenly I wished that I were from Mars
and that Sludge had four tails.
Too late now.
But not too late to go deep
into the woods!

Chapter Four

Found!

"I'm not sure where we are,"
I said to Sludge.
"But neither are the people
who are looking for us."
Sludge wagged his tail.
Sludge was a great detective.
He had been trying to tell me something.
He had wanted to be a bush.

If he had been a bush
and I had been a tree,
we could have easily mixed in with
the real bushes and trees.
But now we had gone deep into the woods
and everybody thought we were lost.
I heard a voice.
Rosamond was talking.
"I will send out a search team of my cats."
I, Nate the Great, did not like to hear that.

Rosamond's cats are the Hexes:
Plain Hex, Little Hex, Big Hex,
and Super Hex.
I hoped they were not hungry.
Claude spoke up.
"I could find Nate if I wanted to,"
he said.
"But today I am not looking
for Nate or Sludge.
I am looking for something special."
Hmmm, I wondered.
Sludge was not wondering.

He was busy sniffing.
He started to walk.
He looked back at me.
"You are a better sniffer than I am,"
I said.
"I'll follow you, Sludge."
Sludge and I zigzagged our way
back to the bench.
Rosamond, Annie, Fang, Claude,
and Harry were waiting.
Rosamond said,
"Nate the Great,
you found yourself.
What a great detective you are."

"No. Sludge is the great detective,"
I said.
"Sludge found us.
He sniffed his way to success."
Sludge licked me.
We sat down on the bench.
It felt good.
Rosamond, Annie, Fang, Claude,
and Harry walked up to the bench.
"We all have cases to solve," Rosamond said.

"I solved Claude's case," I said.
"Just now he found Sludge and me."
Claude stared at me. He was mad.
"You did not solve my case," he said.
"I can find Nate the Great
and Sludge every day.
And now I've found them,
but so what? You are not special."
Annie spoke up.
"My case was the first one,"
she said. "Fang's missing toothpaste.
I rubbed the toothpaste
on his teeth two days ago.
I pressed the tube with my finger
and out came the paste. Very easy."
"How long do Fang's teeth stay shiny?"
I asked.
"Just a few hours," Annie said.
"Very well," I said.
"Let me see Fang's teeth."

Why did I, Nate the Great, say that?
Now I had to look at Fang's teeth.
"They look very shiny," I said.
"How can that be?" I turned to Annie.
"Did Fang like what you did?"
"I don't know," Annie said.
"Fang never looks in the mirror."
"Where did you last see
the toothpaste tube?" I asked.
"On the bathroom counter. Easy to reach.
Someone must have taken it."
I stood up. "Is anyone here brave enough
to clean Fang's teeth?"

Silence.

I, Nate the Great, was not surprised.

"Here is what happened," I said.

"Easy to reach? Well, big Fang could easily have stood up and knocked the toothpaste tube off the counter.

Then he had a good time.

He easily pressed on the tube with his claws.

The paste came out.

Fang easily got his teeth into the toothpaste.

Fang has a shiny smile.
End of case.
I, Nate the Great, say
you will find the toothpaste tube
wherever Fang collects his toys."
Harry raised his hand.

"Can you take my case next?
I'm really scared.
A creature with four tails
ran by me the other day.
It was weird.
It was even wearing a scarf.
I looked in the library
and school for an answer.
But I can't find one.
Four tails. That's a lot."
"Good for you, Harry," I said.

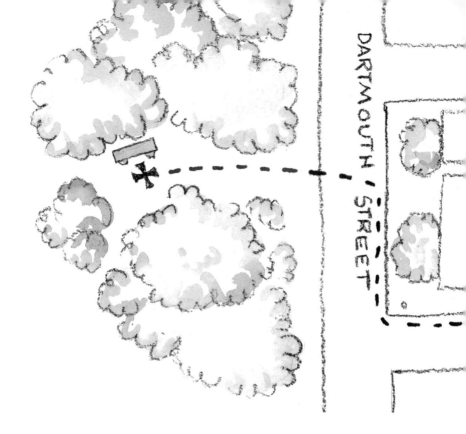

"Looking for information
in a library and school.
Well, I, Nate the Great,
can solve your case right now.
But it's better for you
to see the evidence yourself.
Leave the woods, walk one block
down Dartmouth Street,

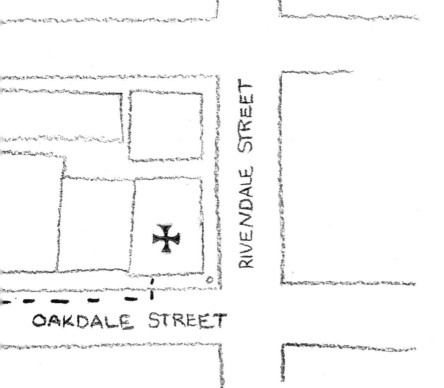

then turn onto Oakdale Street.
Go into the store on the left corner."
"I'll go with Harry," Annie said.
"Sometimes a little brother
needs an older sister."
"Good," Harry said. "Four tails.
That's trouble."
I turned to Sludge.
"We are solving some cases."

"Just a minute," Rosamond said.
"I was Case Number One.
The turnip who walked away.
Remember?"
"How could I forget? I need more pancakes,
and Sludge needs more bones.
We'll have to go home and think.
And think."
"Be sure to watch for the walking turnip,"
Rosamond said.
I, Nate the Great, now knew that
there were worse things
than becoming a man from Mars.

Chapter Five

Where Is the Walking Turnip?

Sludge and I went home.
We looked just like
Sludge and Nate the Great.
And we ate
just like Sludge and Nate the Great.
Everything was the way it should be.
No disguises for us!
I looked at Sludge.
"We did a lot of good detective work today,
didn't we?"
The doorbell rang.

"Not enough," I said.

Rosamond was at the door.

"NATE THE GREAT, WHERE ARE YOU?"

"I'm right here," I said.

"But the turnip isn't," Rosamond said.

"You're a detective,
and you can't find a walking turnip?
I saw you and Sludge go into the
Disguises for Detectives store.
You came out looking just the way
you looked when you walked in.
How boring!"
She stamped her foot and walked away.
I looked at Sludge.

"When we were in the
Disguises for Detectives store,
I should have become a tree,
and you should have become a bush.
You knew that.
When we went into the woods,
nobody would have found us.
Too late now."
Sludge wagged his tail.
He agreed.
"I, Nate the Great,
think that I have a case and a clue.
Somebody was unhappy about
something I said today.
And I think I know
what to do about it."

Chapter Six
Happy Endings

"**W**e are going to Claude's house," I said.
Sludge and I took the last bites of our food.
Then we rushed to Claude's house.
I knocked on his door.
Claude opened it.
"Well, hello, Nate the Great and Sludge."
Claude looked mad.
He kept talking.
"You should know that finding you two
is not special," he said.
"I can find you any time I want.

I know where you live.
I know what you eat.
But that's not special enough for today.
Today I want to find something
really special."
Sludge looked sad.
He thought he was special.
Claude looked straight at me.
"Do you know what's really special to find?
It's a walking turnip."

"I, Nate the Great, say that a walking turnip
isn't special because there is
no such thing as a walking turnip."
Claude looked proud.
"Well, I just saw one," he said,
"and now I'm a very happy Claude."
"Glad to hear that," I said.
"I, Nate the Great, like happy endings
in a case, and so . . . congratulations!"
Sludge and I left Claude's house.
This case was not over.

Chapter Seven

The Walking Turnip Is Found!

I, Nate the Great, and Sludge
did something we don't like to do.
We walked to Rosamond's house.
I rang her doorbell.
She was home.
I heard her coming to the door.
Sludge and I walked into her house.
"Why are you here?"
Rosamond asked.
"I, Nate the Great, have good news."
"Oh?" Rosamond said. "What good news?"

I smiled. "I found the walking turnip.
Exactly what you wanted me to do."

"Well, um . . . ," Rosamond said.

"Why don't you like this news?" I asked.
"You were angry that I hadn't found
the turnip."

"Well, um . . . ," Rosamond said.

Sludge and I walked straight
up to Rosamond.

"You," I said, "are the walking turnip."

"How do you know that?" she asked.

"I put some clues together," I said.
"You knew about the disguise store
and you thought it would be fun
to dress up as a turnip.
You bought a turnip costume.
Claude told you that he wanted
to find something special today.
So you pretended that you had
a real problem about a walking turnip.

And when you got a chance,
you walked in your tall turnip costume
in front of Claude. Now he's very happy.
And you are still pretending that you are
looking for a walking turnip.
You did a nice thing for Claude.
It is not exactly what Sludge
and I would have done."
Sludge wagged his tail.
Rosamond actually smiled.

"I was getting tired of saying that I was
looking for a walking turnip," she said.
"Glad to be of help," I said.
Sludge and I went home.

Chapter Eight

Forever Great

"Let's sit down and talk," I said to Sludge.
"People who pretend to be
something they are not
should not do that
unless it's Halloween
or they are at a costume party.
But I never want to be a man from Mars.
I don't want to be a tree.
And I don't want my dog to be a bush.
Okay?"

Sludge jumped on my lap.
And we sat and thought
how great it was
to be forever
Nate the Great and Sludge.